Animal Fun Facts

FUN FACTS ABOUT BEARS

by Julie Murray

Dash!
LEVELED READERS
An Imprint of Abdo Zoom • abdobooks.com

2

Dash!
LEVELED READERS

Level 1 – Beginning
Short and simple sentences with familiar words or patterns for children who are beginning to understand how letters and sounds go together.

Level 2 – Emerging
Longer words and sentences with more complex language patterns for readers who are practicing common words and letter sounds.

Level 3 – Transitional
More developed language and vocabulary for readers who are becoming more independent.

THIS BOOK CONTAINS RECYCLED MATERIALS

abdobooks.com

Published by Abdo Zoom, a division of ABDO, PO Box 398166, Minneapolis, Minnesota 55439.

Printed in the United States of America, North Mankato, Minnesota.
052021
092021

Photo Credits: iStock, Minden Pictures, Shutterstock
Production Contributors: Kenny Abdo, Jennie Forsberg, Grace Hansen, John Hansen
Design Contributors: Candice Keimig, Neil Klinepier

Library of Congress Control Number: 2020919483

Publisher's Cataloging in Publication Data

Names: Murray, Julie, author.
Title: Fun facts about bears / by Julie Murray
Description: Minneapolis, Minnesota : Abdo Zoom, 2022 | Series: Animal fun facts | Includes online resources and index.
Identifiers: ISBN 9781098224455 (lib. bdg.) | ISBN 9781098225391 (ebook) | ISBN 9781098225865 (Read-to-Me ebook)
Subjects: LCSH: Bears--Juvenile literature. | Bears--Behavior--Juvenile literature. | Questions and answers--Juvenile literature. | Animal behavior--Juvenile literature.
Classification: DDC 599.78--dc23

Table of Contents

Fun Facts About Bears

There are eight **species** of bears. Black bears, brown bears, and polar bears are all found in North America.

Asiatic bears spend a lot of time in trees. They even make nests in trees to sleep!

Some bears do not go to the bathroom while they **hibernate**. Instead, their bodies change waste into **protein**. This helps them keep their muscles.

Panda bears spend most of their day eating. They eat 50 to 60 pounds (22.7 to 27.2 kg) of **bamboo** each day!

The sloth bear's name can be misleading. It is not slow like a sloth. It can run faster than a human.

Not all black bears are black in color. Some are brown, gray, or even cream.

A grizzly bear has a hump on its back. This is a large muscle. The bear uses this muscle to dig for food and dig out its den.

The smallest bear is the sun bear. It weighs up to 150 pounds (68 kg). It is half the size of an American black bear.

The largest bear on average is the polar bear. Males can grow up to 9 feet (2.7 m) long. They can weigh up to 1,600 pounds (725.7 kg)!

Animal Spotlight

Giant Pandas

Size: Up to 6 feet (1.8 m) long; Up to 330 pounds (149.7 kg)

Appearance: black and white coat, small eyes surrounded by black fur, and round, black ears.

Range: mountain regions of southwestern China

Habitat: mainly temperate forests high in the mountains

Diet: bamboo shoots and leaves

Status: vulnerable

Glossary

bamboo – a tropical plant that has hard, woody, hallow stems.

hibernate – to sleep through the winter in a den or burrow to save energy.

protein – a substance that is found in all living things and that is a necessary part of life processes.

species – a group of living things that look alike, share a common name, and can have young with one another.

Index

Online Resources

Booklinks
NONFICTION NETWORK
FREE! ONLINE NONFICTION RESOURCES

To learn more about bears, please visit **abdobooklinks.com** or scan this QR code. These links are routinely monitored and updated to provide the most current information available.